A Note to Parents and Caregivers:

Read-it! Readers are for children who are just starting on the amazing road to reading. These beautiful books support both the acquisition of reading skills and the love of books.

The RED LEVEL presents familiar topics using common words and repeating sentence patterns.

The BLUE LEVEL presents new ideas using a larger vocabulary and varied sentence structure.

The YELLOW LEVEL presents more challenging ideas, a broad vocabulary, and wide variety in sentence structure.

The GREEN LEVEL presents more complex ideas, an extended vocabulary range, and expanded language structures.

When sharing a book with your child, read in short stretches, pausing often to talk about the pictures. Have your child turn the pages and point to the pictures and familiar words. And be sure to reread favorite stories or parts of stories.

There is no right or wrong way to share books with children. Find time to read with your child, and pass on the legacy of literacy.

Adria F. Klein, Ph.D.
Professor Emeritus
California State University
San Bernardino, California

Editor: Bob Temple
Creative Director: Terri Foley
Editorial Adviser: Andrea Cascardi
Copy Editor: Laurie Kahn
Designer: Melissa Voda
Page production: The Design Lab
The illustrations in this book were painted with gouache.

Picture Window Books
5115 Excelsior Boulevard
Suite 232
Minneapolis, MN 55416
1-877-845-8392
www.picturewindowbooks.com

Printed in the United States of America.

Library of Congress Cataloging-in-Publication Data
White, Mark.
The goose that laid the golden egg : a retelling of Aesop's fable / written by
Mark White ; illustrated by Sara Rojo.
p. cm. — (Read-it! Readers Fables)
Summary: A farmer learns a lesson in greed when one of his geese begins
to lay one—and only one—golden egg each day.
ISBN 1-4048-0219-3
[1. Folklore. 2. Fables.] I. Rojo, Sara, ill. II. Aesop. III. Title. IV. Series.
PZ8.2.W55 Go 2004
398.2452—dc21   2003006300

PICTURE WINDOW BOOKS
Minneapolis, Minnesota

Read-it! Readers
Blue Level

The Goose that Laid the Golden Egg

A Retelling of Aesop's Fable

Written by Mark White

Illustrated by Sara Rojo

Library Adviser:
Kathy Baxter, M.A.
Former Coordinator of Children's Services
Anoka County (Minnesota) Library

Reading Advisers:
Adria F. Klein, Ph.D.
Professor Emeritus, California State University
San Bernardino, California

Susan Kesselring, M.A.
Literacy Educator
Rosemount-Apple Valley-Eagan (Minnesota) School District

Picture Window Books
Minneapolis, Minnesota

There was once a very special goose.

She looked like other geese.
Her neck was long and slender.
Her feathers were fluffy and white.
Her beak and feet were orange.

But she wasn't like the other geese.
The eggs she laid were solid gold!

The farmer was very excited when he found the first golden egg. He sold the pretty egg for a lot of money.

10

The farmer had many geese.
He collected all of the goose eggs
every morning.

Each day the farmer found
the special goose had laid
one golden egg.

The farmer sold the special eggs
in town.

Soon he was rich from selling
the golden eggs.

The farmer was greedy.
He wanted to be richer.
He wanted more than just
one golden egg each day.

18

The farmer tried to make
the other geese lay golden eggs
like the special goose did.

He tried to make the special goose
lay more than one egg each day.

But nothing worked.

The special goose still laid just
one golden egg every morning.
The other geese still laid
their normal eggs.

The farmer had one more idea.
He decided to kill the goose.
Then he could take all
the special eggs at once!
The farmer went to the barn
and killed the goose.

But inside, she was just like
the other geese.

The farmer sat down and cried.
One golden egg each day
had not been enough for him.
Now he would have none.

24

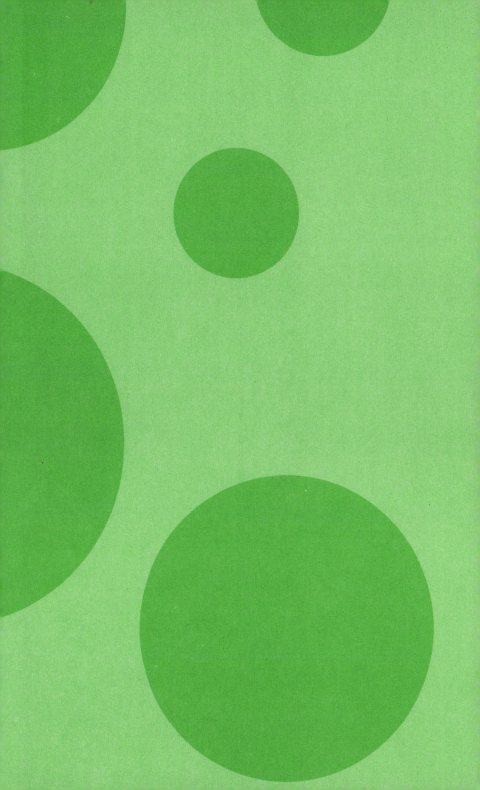